Animal Trainer

By Susan Koehler
Cover Illustrated By Ken Hooper
Cover Color By Lance Borde
Interior Illustrated By Thomas Zahler

ROURKE PUBLISHING

Vero Beach, Florida 32964

www.rourkepublishing.com

Edited by Katherine M. Thal and Meg Greve
Cover Illustrated By Ken Hooper
Cover Color By Lance Bord
Interior Illustrated by Thomas Zahler
Art Direction and Page Layout by Renee Brady

Photo Credits: c-foto © pg. 1, 3-4, 26-32; Franky DeMeyer © pg. 26; U.S. Marine Corps © pg. 27; bobbymn © pg. 28; Dan Dee Shots © pg. 28

Library of Congress Cataloging-in-Publication Data

Koehler, Susan, 1963-
  Animal trainer / Susan Koehler.
      p. cm. -- (Jobs that rock gaphic illustrated)
  Includes bibliographical references and index.
  ISBN 978-1-60694-376-2 (Hardcover) (alk. paper)
  ISBN 978-1-60694-559-9 (Softcover)
  1. Animal training--Comic books, strips, etc. 2. Animal training--Vocational guidance--Juvenile literature. 3. Animal trainers--Juvenile literature. I. Title.
  GV1829.K64 2010
  636.08'35--dc22

                              2009020486

Rourke Publishing
Printed in the United States of America, North Mankato, Minnesota
062310
062210LP-A

www.rourkepublishing.com - rourke@rourkepublishing.com
Post Office Box 643328 Vero Beach, Florida 32964

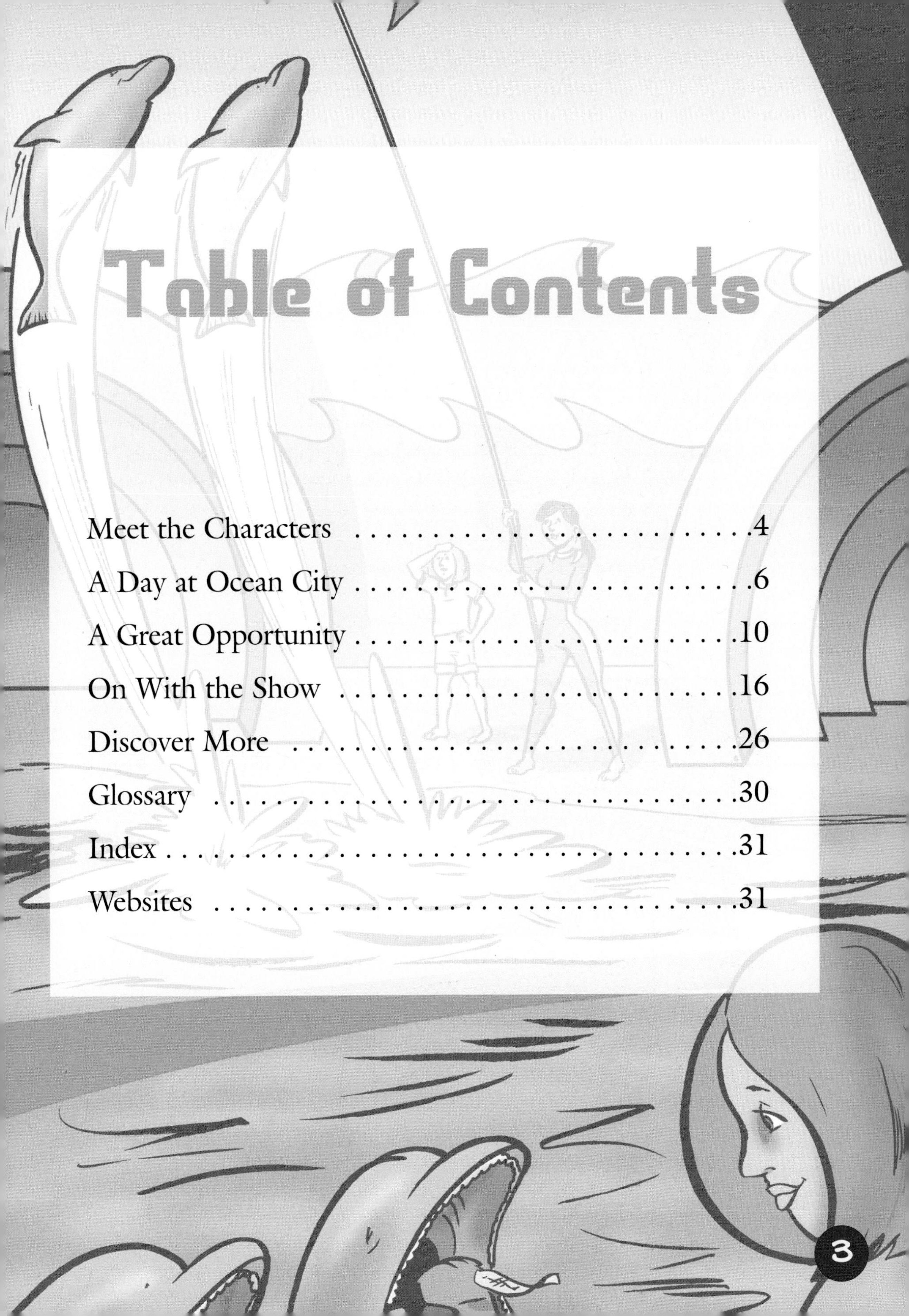

Table of Contents

Hillary Fischer

Hillary Fischer is a nine-year-old girl with a cousin who is a dolphin trainer.

Grandma

Hillary's grandmother takes her to watch a dolphin show at Ocean City.

Emily Fisher

Emily is Hillary's cousin, a dolphin trainer at Ocean City.

Uncle John

Uncle John is Emily's father and the head veterinarian at Ocean City.

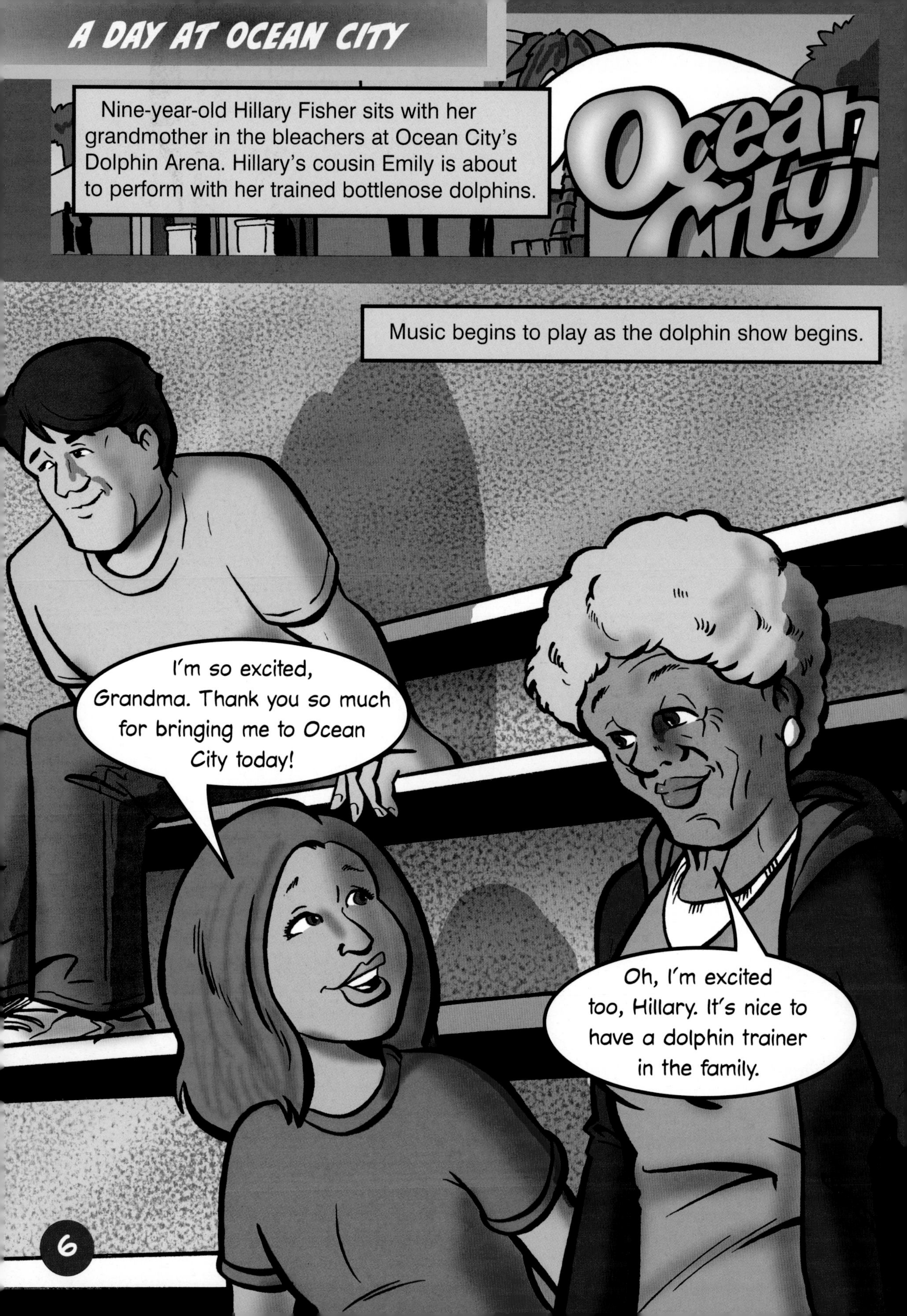
A DAY AT OCEAN CITY
Nine-year-old Hillary Fisher sits with her grandmother in the bleachers at Ocean City's Dolphin Arena. Hillary's cousin Emily is about to perform with her trained bottlenose dolphins.
Ocean City
Music begins to play as the dolphin show begins.
I'm so excited, Grandma. Thank you so much for bringing me to Ocean City today!
Oh, I'm excited too, Hillary. It's nice to have a dolphin trainer in the family.

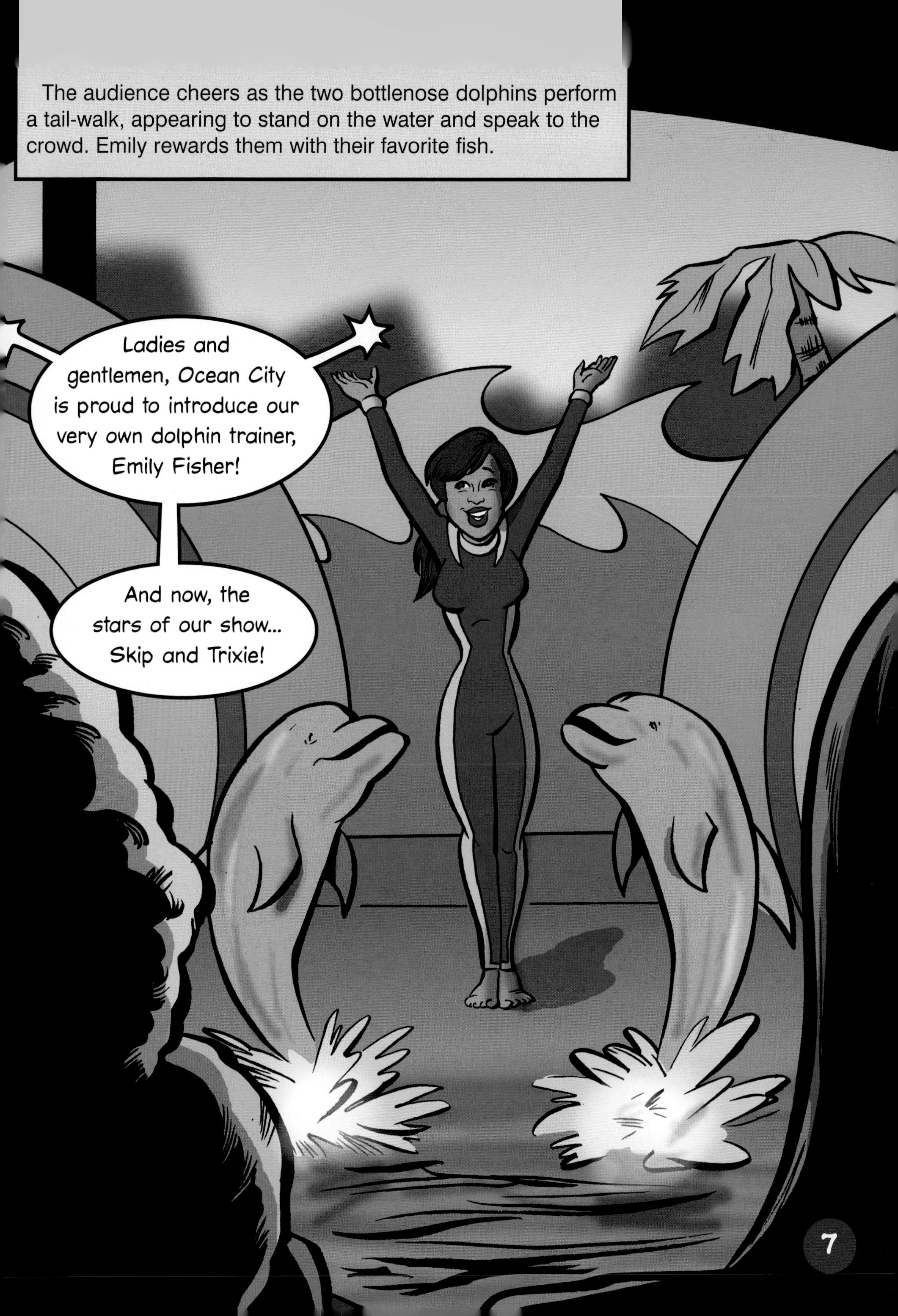
The audience cheers as the two bottlenose dolphins perform a tail-walk, appearing to stand on the water and speak to the crowd. Emily rewards them with their favorite fish.
Ladies and gentlemen, Ocean City is proud to introduce our very own dolphin trainer, Emily Fisher!
And now, the stars of our show... Skip and Trixie!

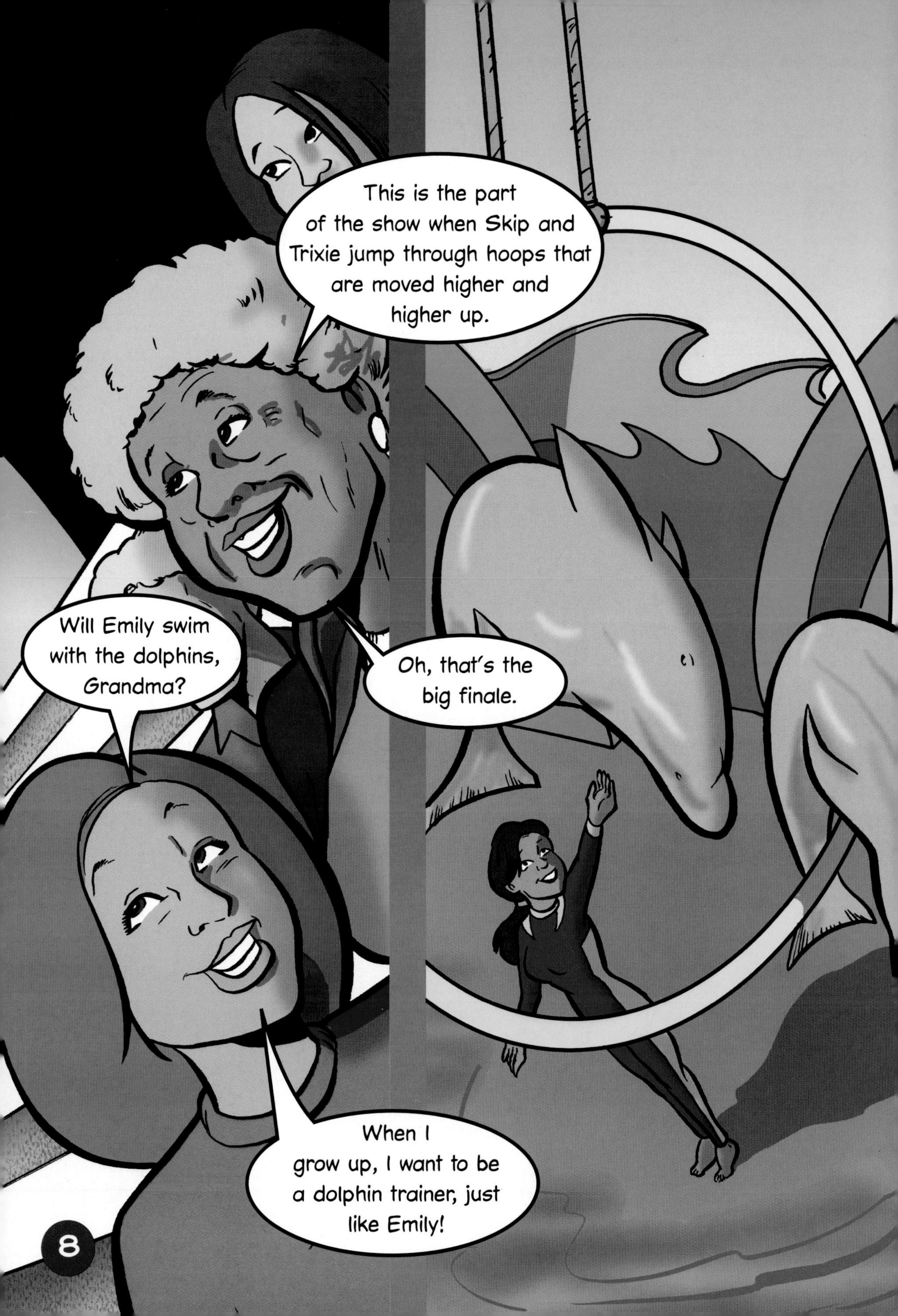
This is the part of the show when Skip and Trixie jump through hoops that are moved higher and higher up.
Will Emily swim with the dolphins, Grandma?
Oh, that's the big finale.
When I grow up, I want to be a dolphin trainer, just like Emily!

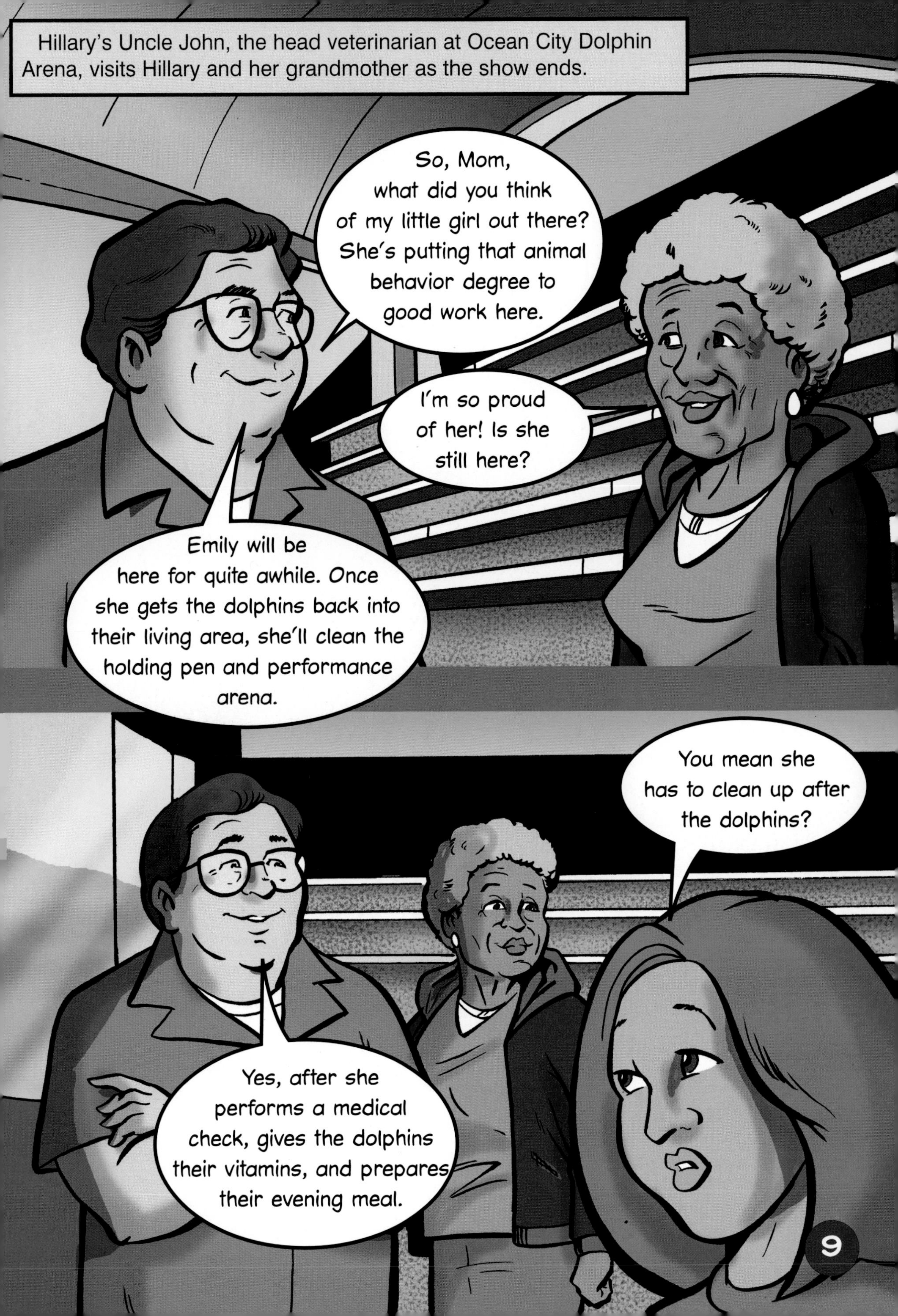
Hillary's Uncle John, the head veterinarian at Ocean City Dolphin Arena, visits Hillary and her grandmother as the show ends.
So, Mom, what did you think of my little girl out there? She's putting that animal behavior degree to good work here.
I'm so proud of her! Is she still here?
Emily will be here for quite awhile. Once she gets the dolphins back into their living area, she'll clean the holding pen and performance arena.
You mean she has to clean up after the dolphins?
Yes, after she performs a medical check, gives the dolphins their vitamins, and prepares their evening meal.

A GREAT OPPORTUNITY

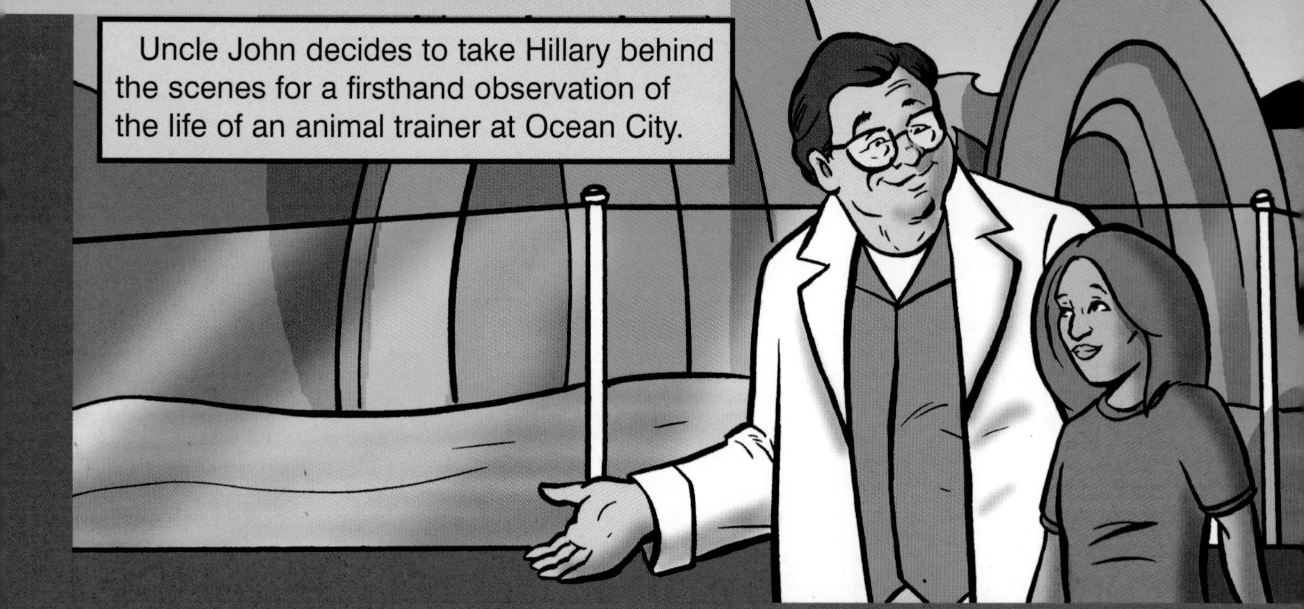
Uncle John decides to take Hillary behind the scenes for a firsthand observation of the life of an animal trainer at Ocean City.

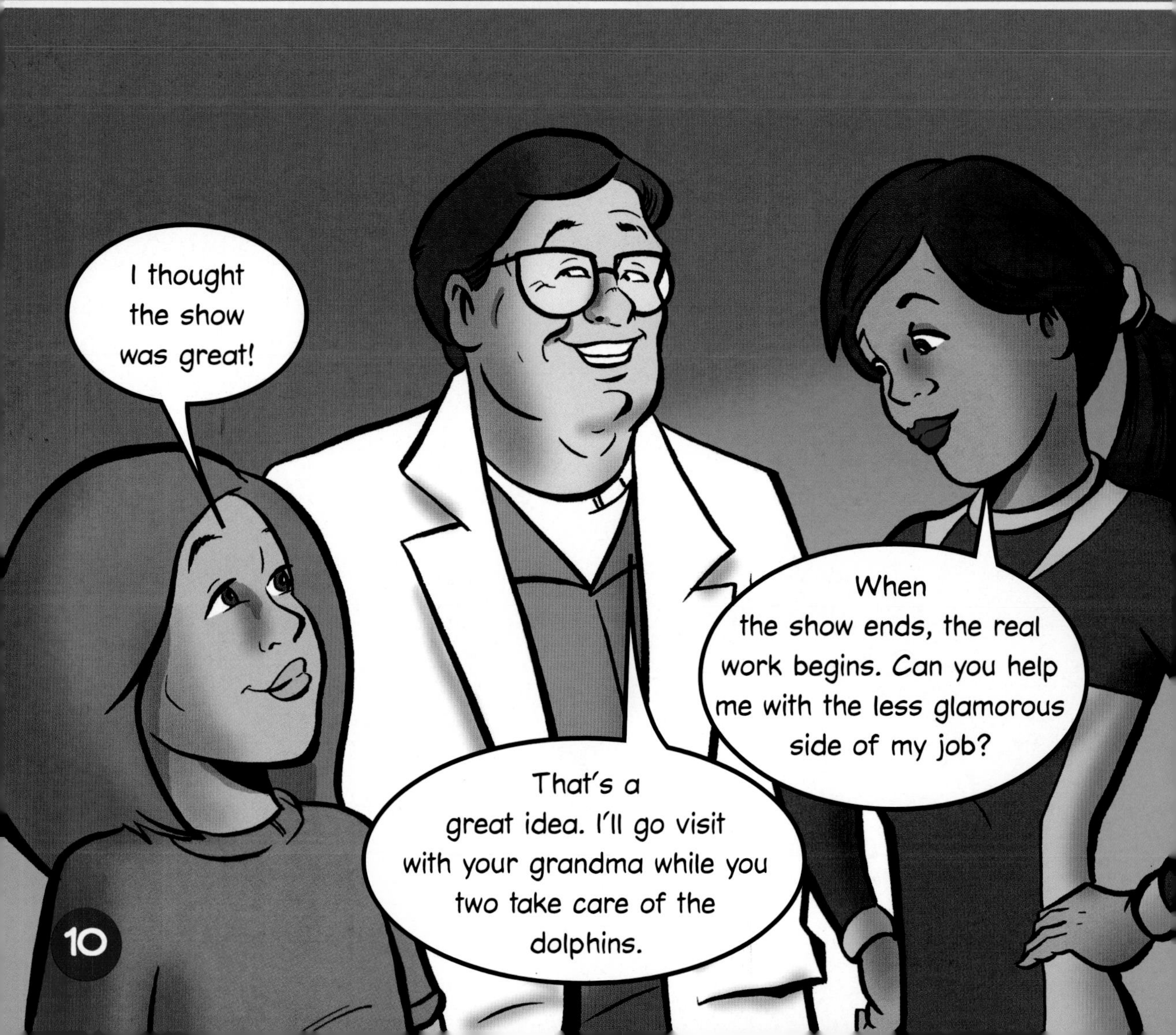
I thought the show was great!
When the show ends, the real work begins. Can you help me with the less glamorous side of my job?
That's a great idea. I'll go visit with your grandma while you two take care of the dolphins.

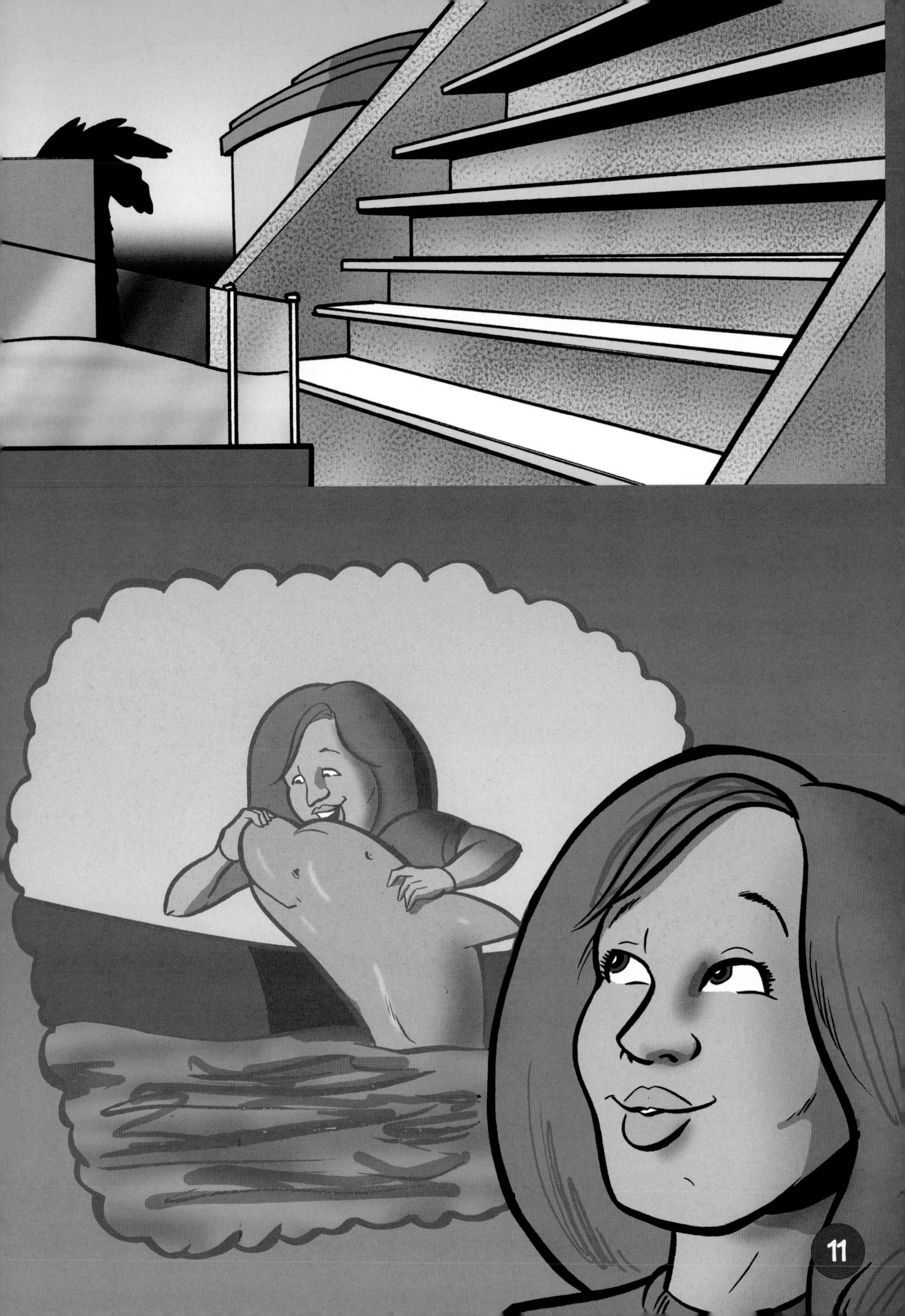

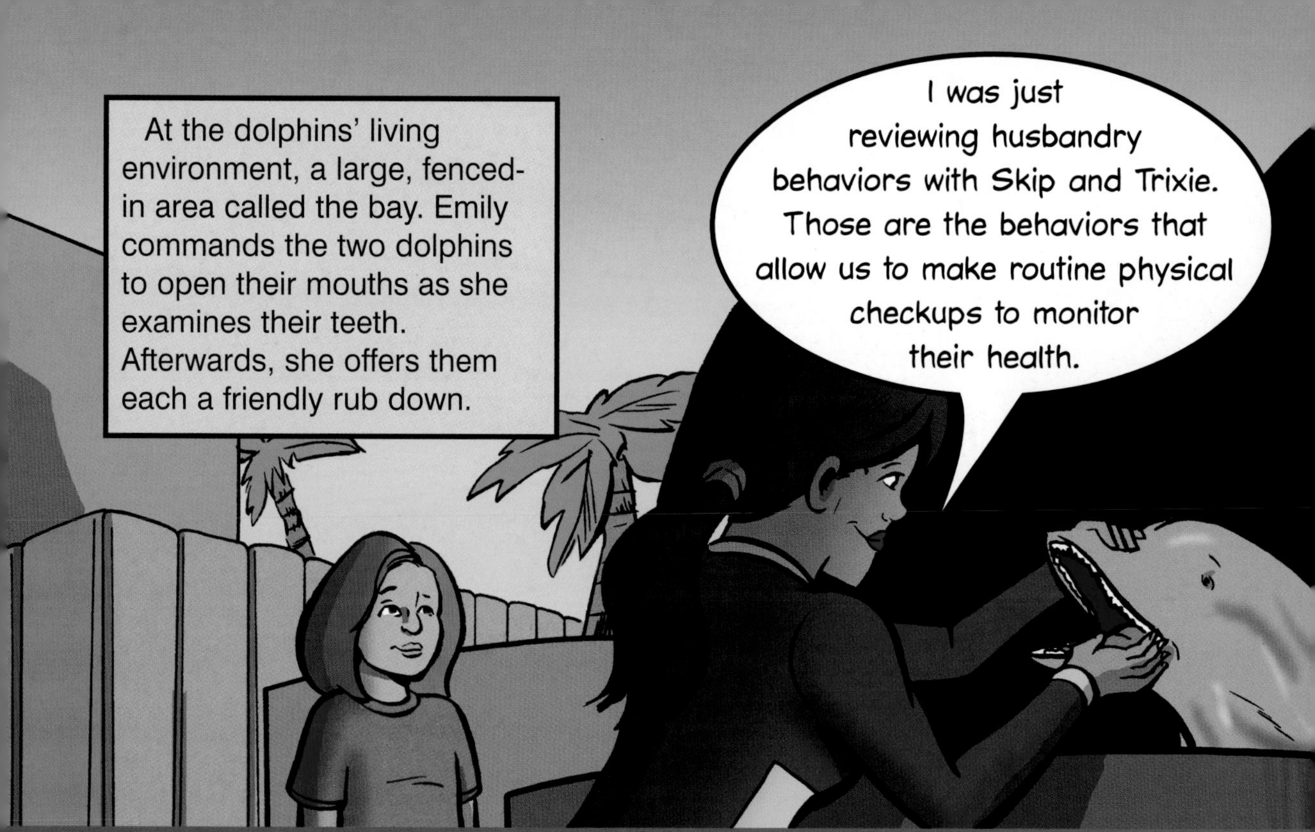
At the dolphins' living environment, a large, fenced-in area called the bay. Emily commands the two dolphins to open their mouths as she examines their teeth. Afterwards, she offers them each a friendly rub down.
I was just reviewing husbandry behaviors with Skip and Trixie. Those are the behaviors that allow us to make routine physical checkups to monitor their health.

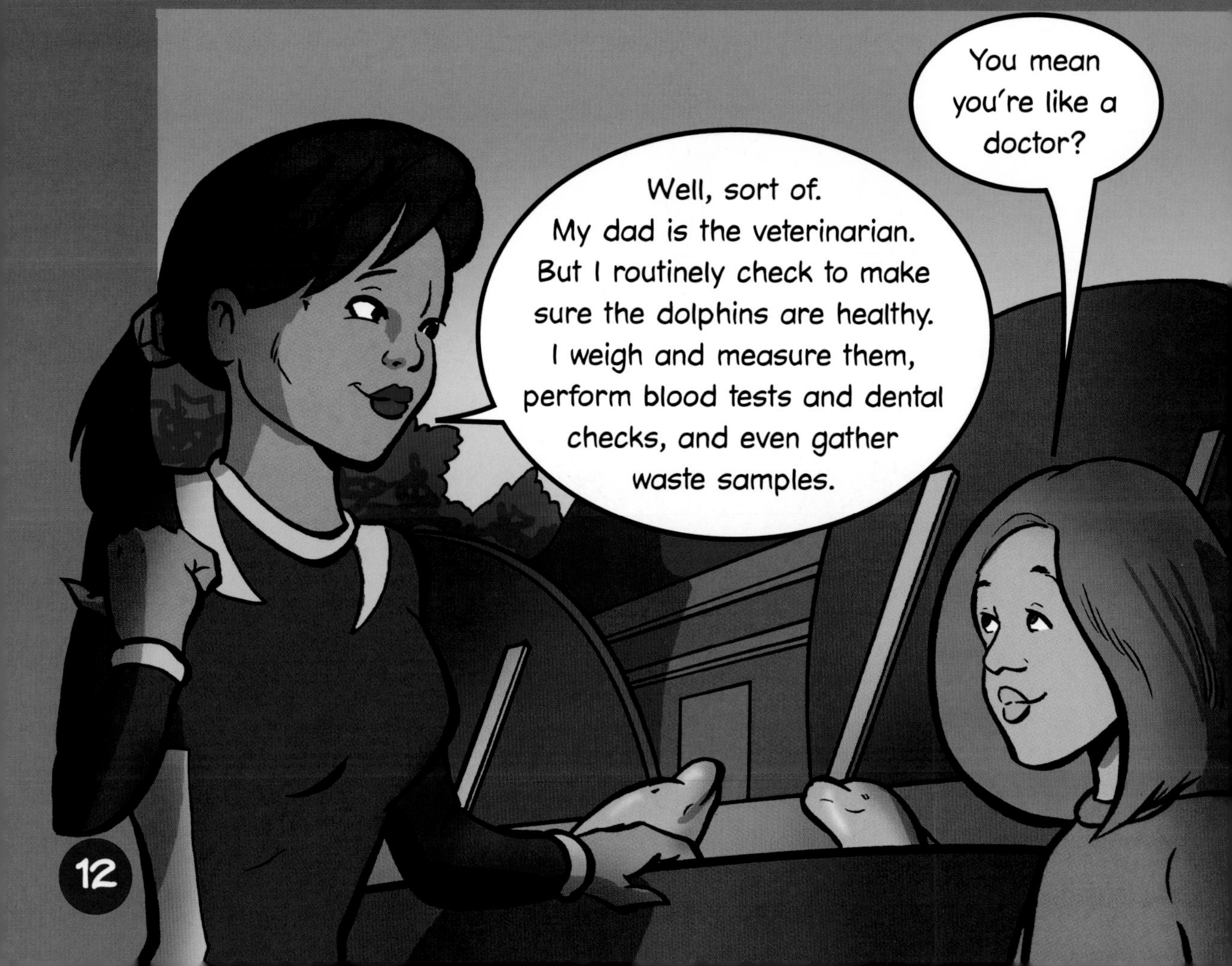
You mean you're like a doctor?
Well, sort of. My dad is the veterinarian. But I routinely check to make sure the dolphins are healthy. I weigh and measure them, perform blood tests and dental checks, and even gather waste samples.

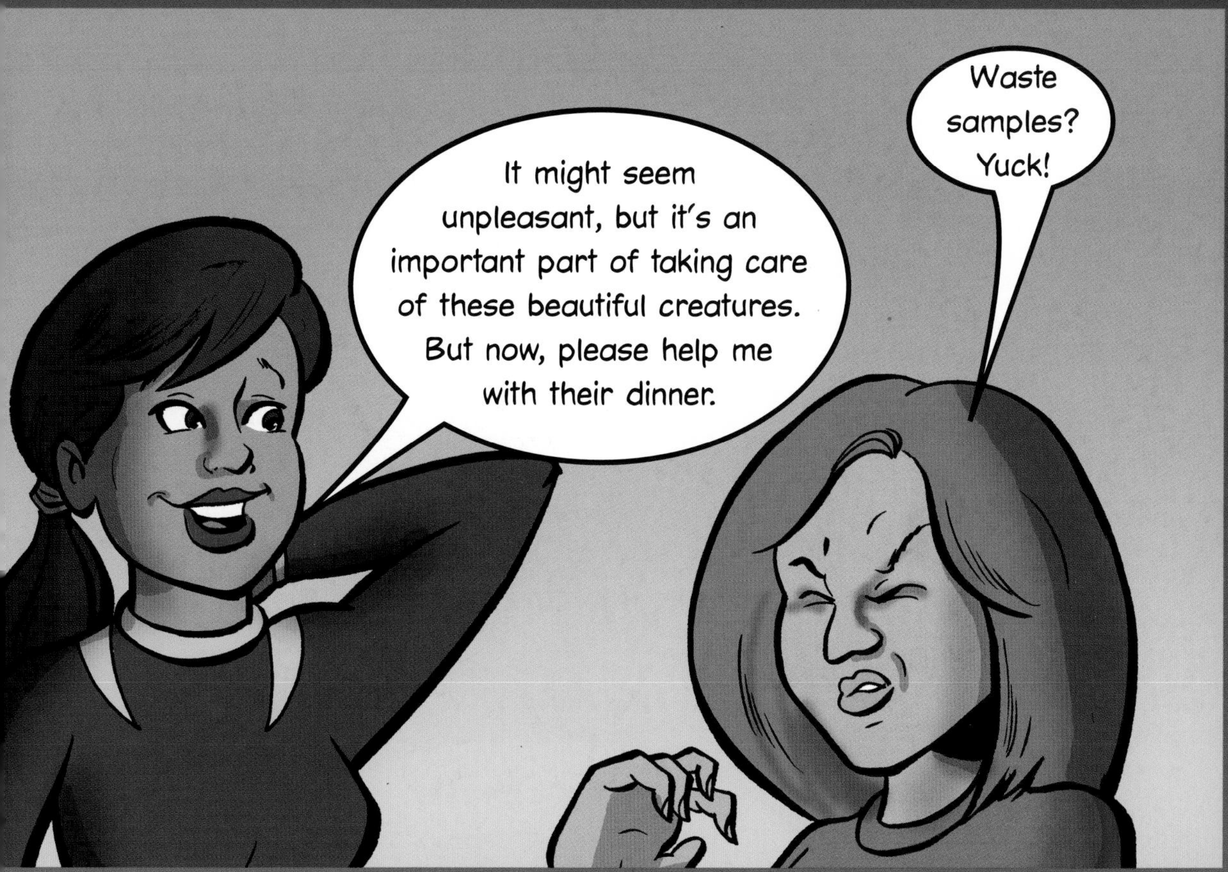
It might seem unpleasant, but it's an important part of taking care of these beautiful creatures. But now, please help me with their dinner.
Waste samples? Yuck!

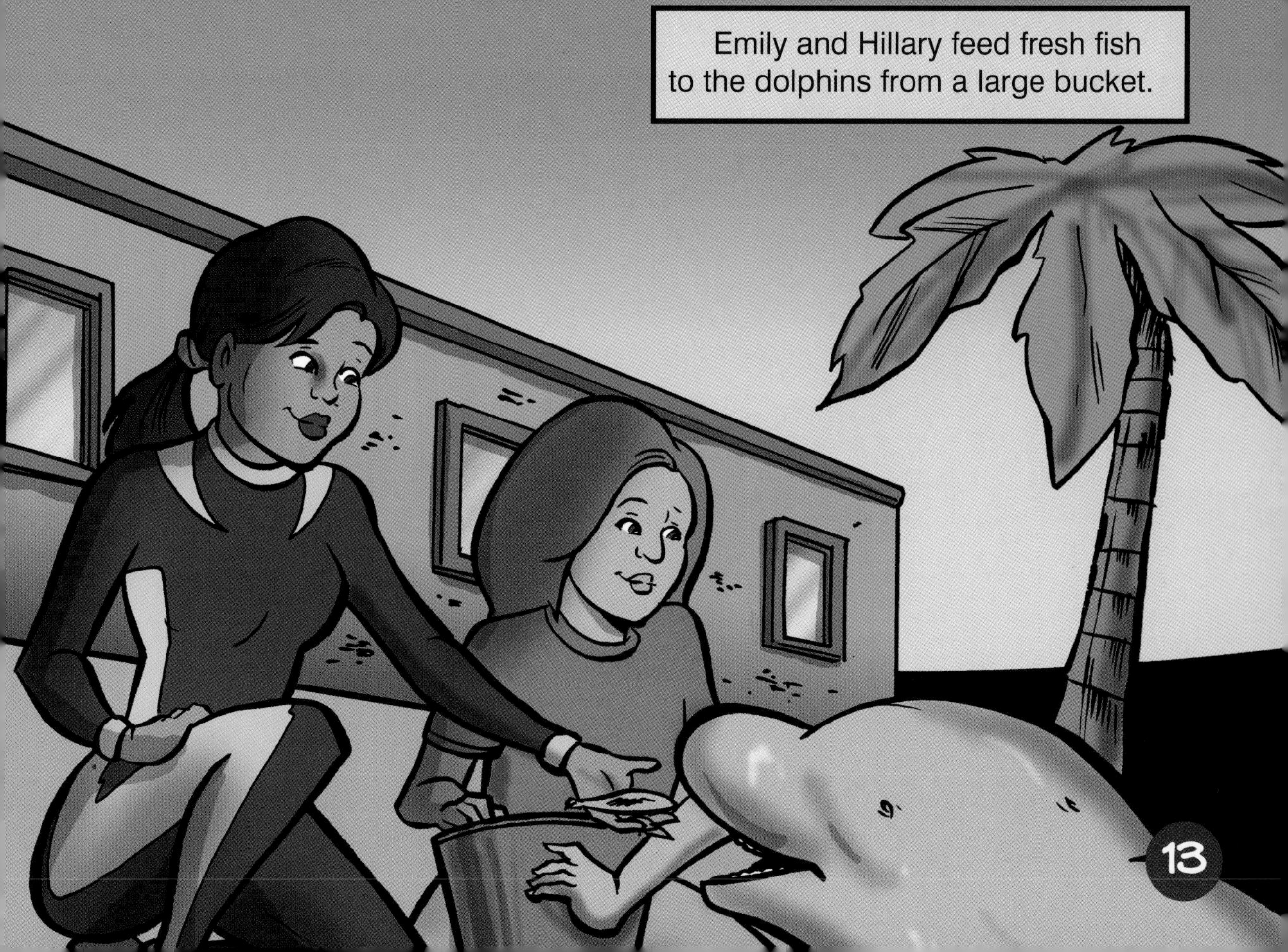
Emily and Hillary feed fresh fish to the dolphins from a large bucket.

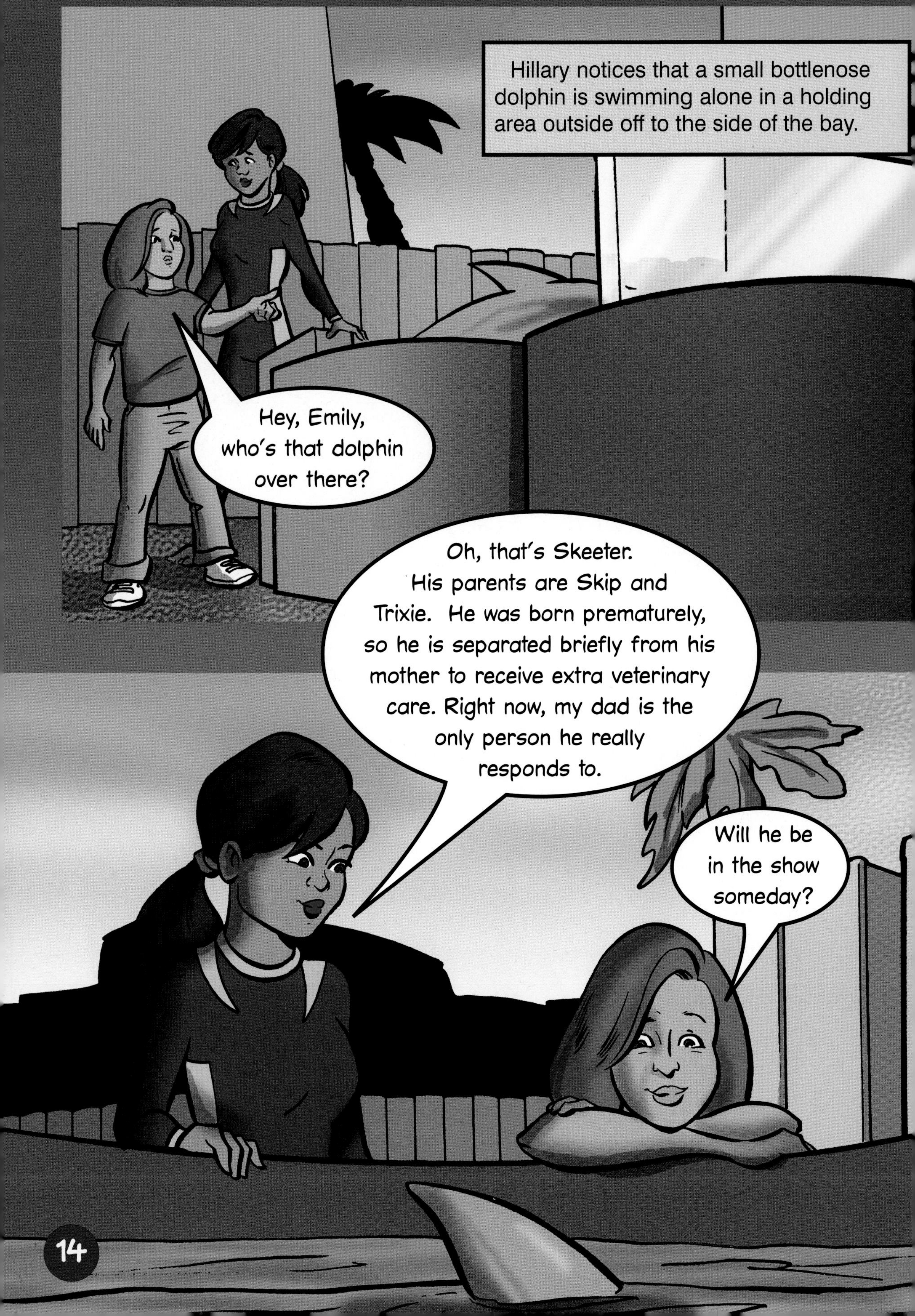
Hillary notices that a small bottlenose dolphin is swimming alone in a holding area outside off to the side of the bay.
Hey, Emily, who's that dolphin over there?
Oh, that's Skeeter. His parents are Skip and Trixie. He was born prematurely, so he is separated briefly from his mother to receive extra veterinary care. Right now, my dad is the only person he really responds to.
Will he be in the show someday?

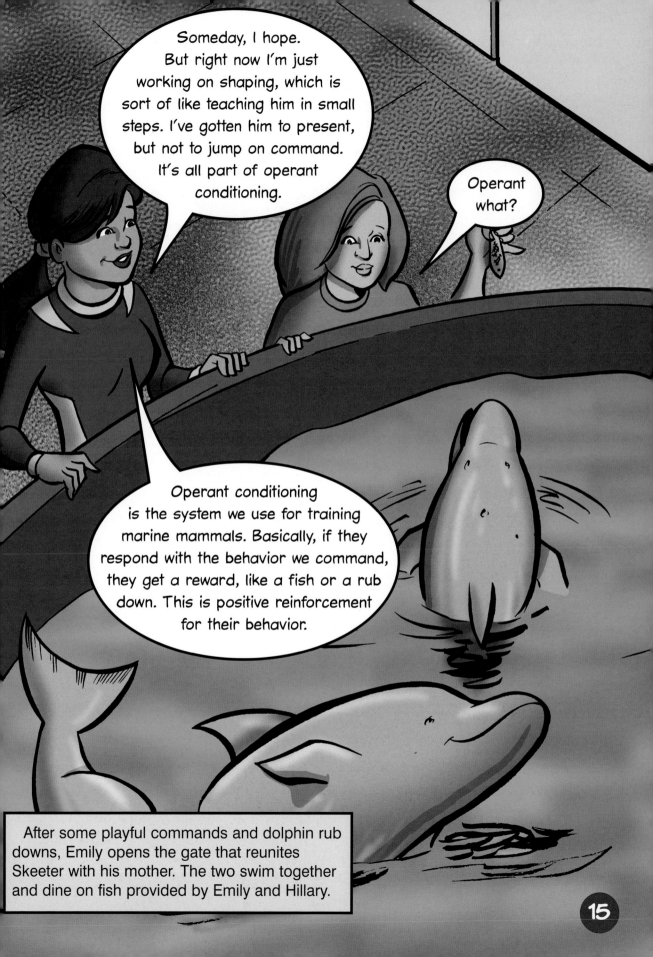

Someday, I hope. But right now I'm just working on shaping, which is sort of like teaching him in small steps. I've gotten him to present, but not to jump on command. It's all part of operant conditioning.

Operant what?

Operant conditioning is the system we use for training marine mammals. Basically, if they respond with the behavior we command, they get a reward, like a fish or a rub down. This is positive reinforcement for their behavior.

After some playful commands and dolphin rub downs, Emily opens the gate that reunites Skeeter with his mother. The two swim together and dine on fish provided by Emily and Hillary.

ON WITH THE SHOW

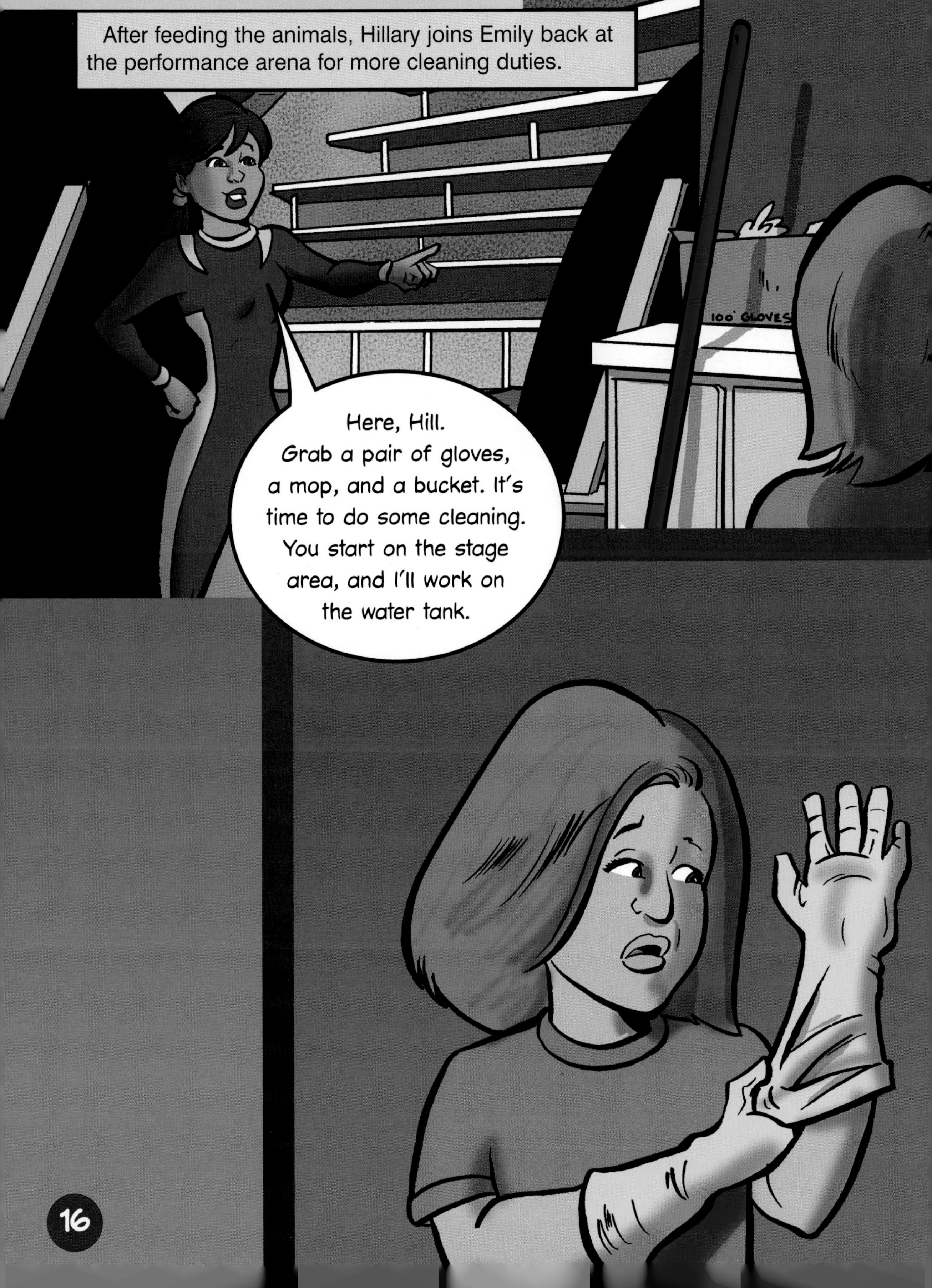
After feeding the animals, Hillary joins Emily back at the performance arena for more cleaning duties.
100 GLOVES
Here, Hill. Grab a pair of gloves, a mop, and a bucket. It's time to do some cleaning. You start on the stage area, and I'll work on the water tank.

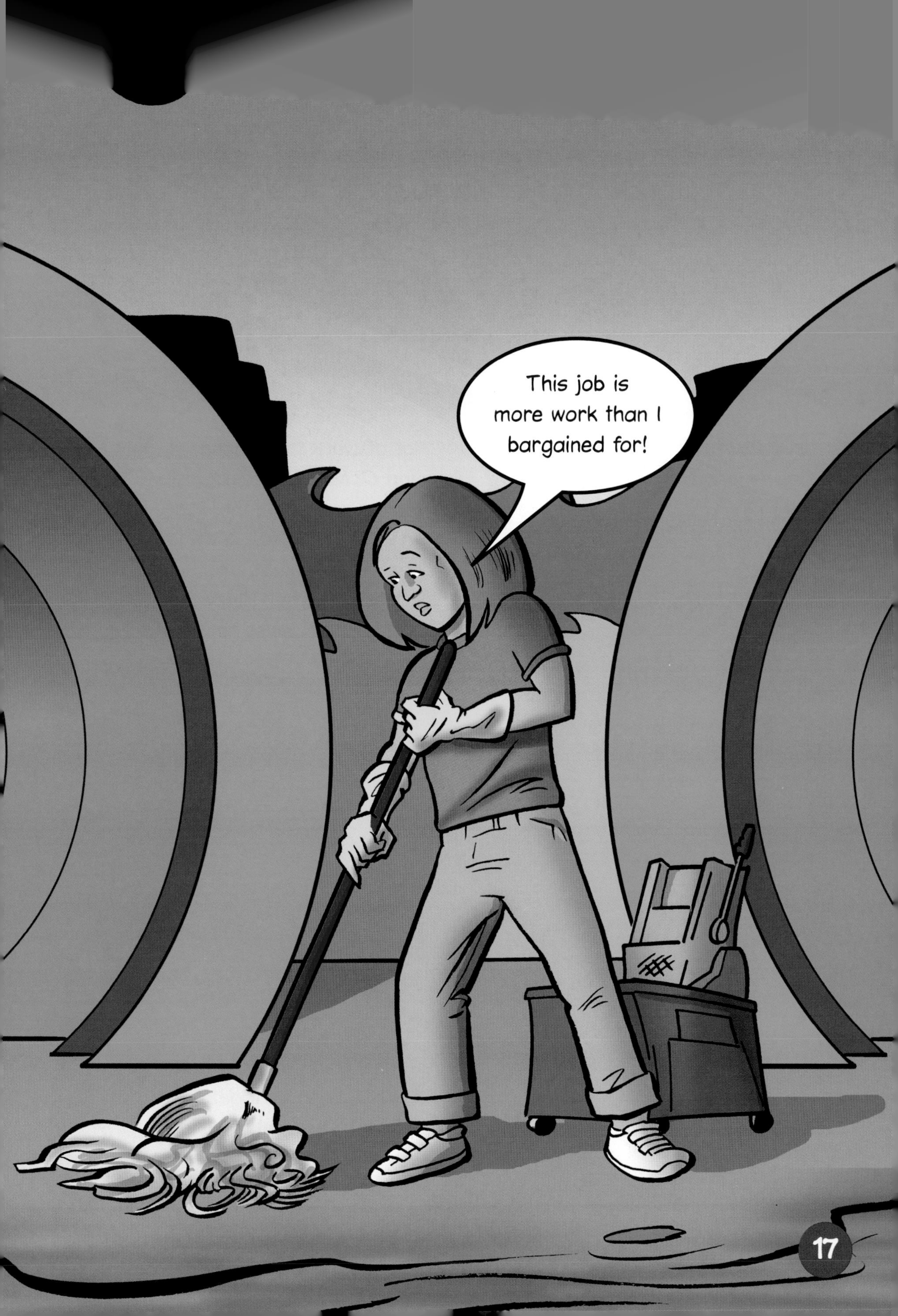
This job is more work than I bargained for!

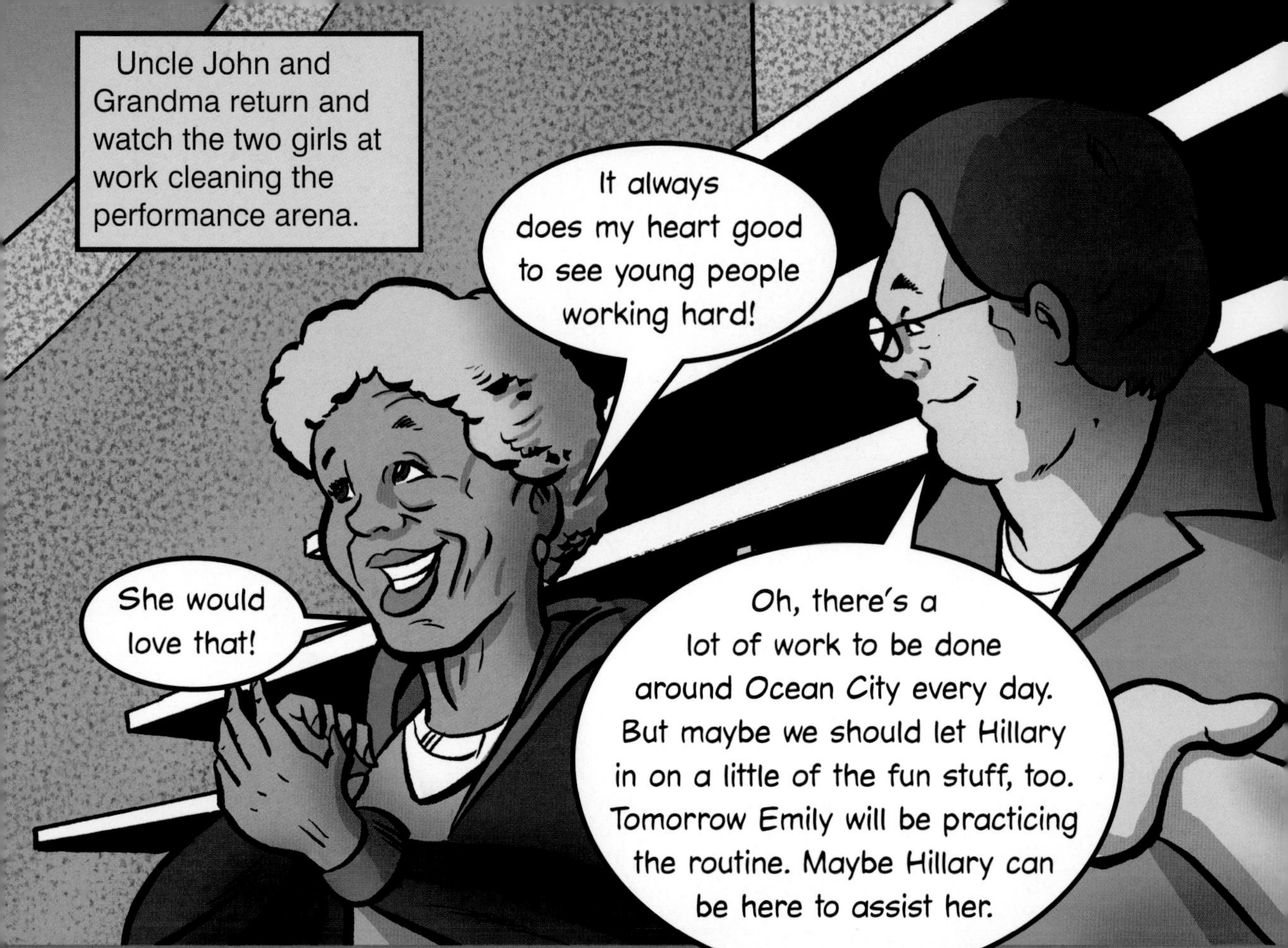
Uncle John and Grandma return and watch the two girls at work cleaning the performance arena.
It always does my heart good to see young people working hard!
Oh, there's a lot of work to be done around Ocean City every day. But maybe we should let Hillary in on a little of the fun stuff, too. Tomorrow Emily will be practicing the routine. Maybe Hillary can be here to assist her.
She would love that!

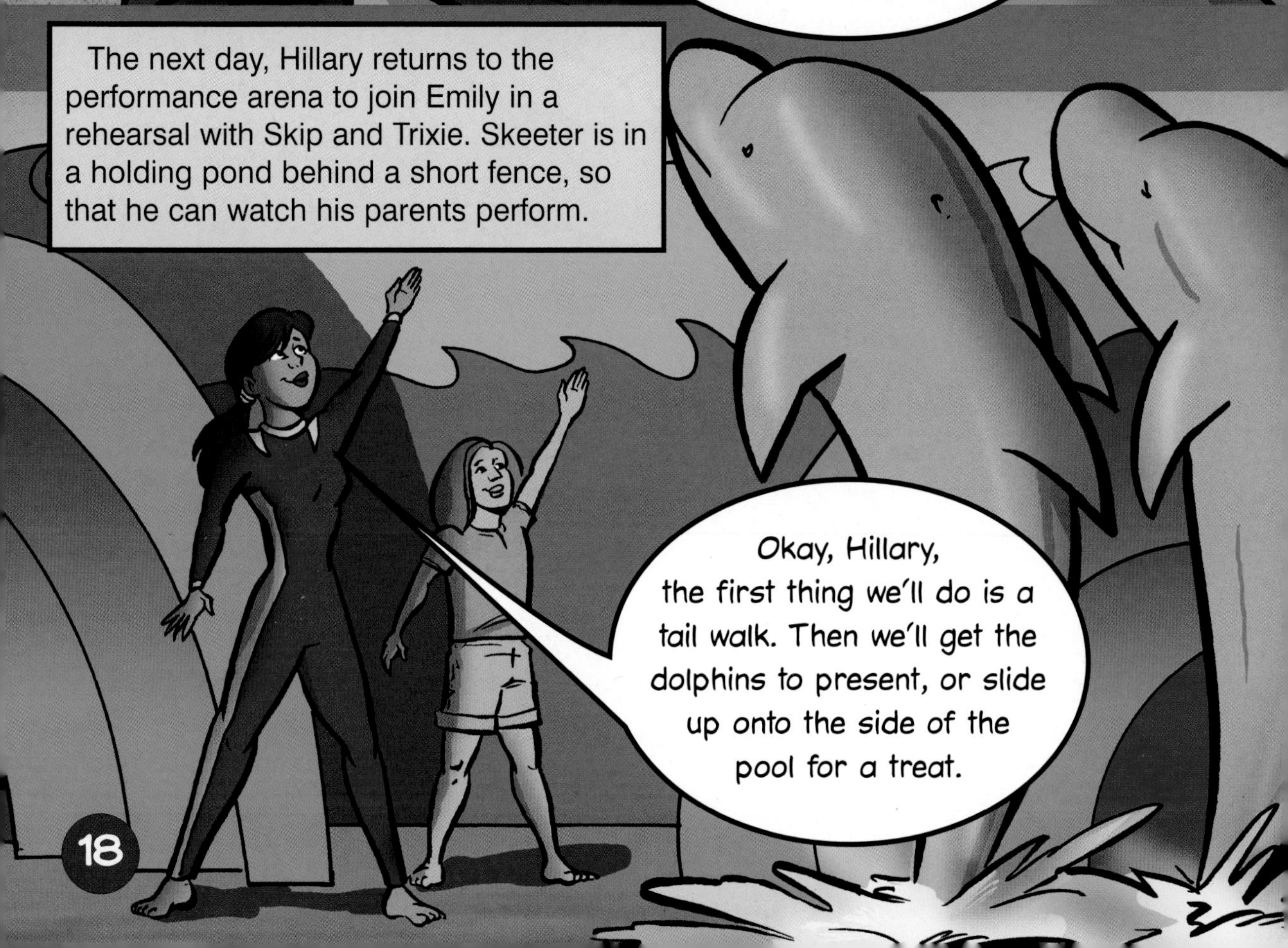
The next day, Hillary returns to the performance arena to join Emily in a rehearsal with Skip and Trixie. Skeeter is in a holding pond behind a short fence, so that he can watch his parents perform.
Okay, Hillary, the first thing we'll do is a tail walk. Then we'll get the dolphins to present, or slide up onto the side of the pool for a treat.

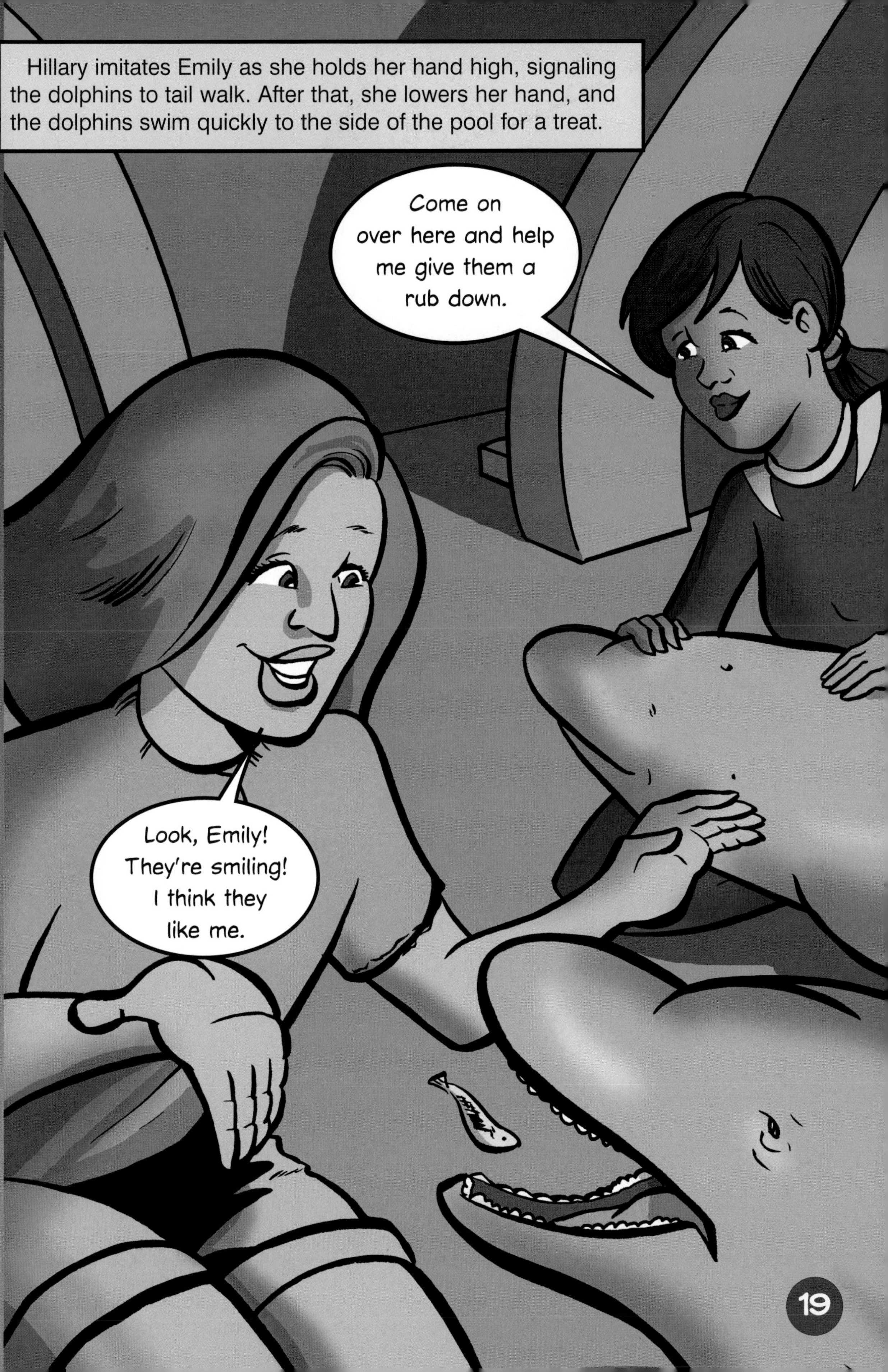
Hillary imitates Emily as she holds her hand high, signaling the dolphins to tail walk. After that, she lowers her hand, and the dolphins swim quickly to the side of the pool for a treat.
Come on over here and help me give them a rub down.
Look, Emily! They're smiling! I think they like me.

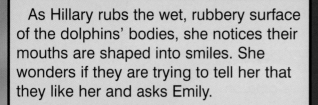

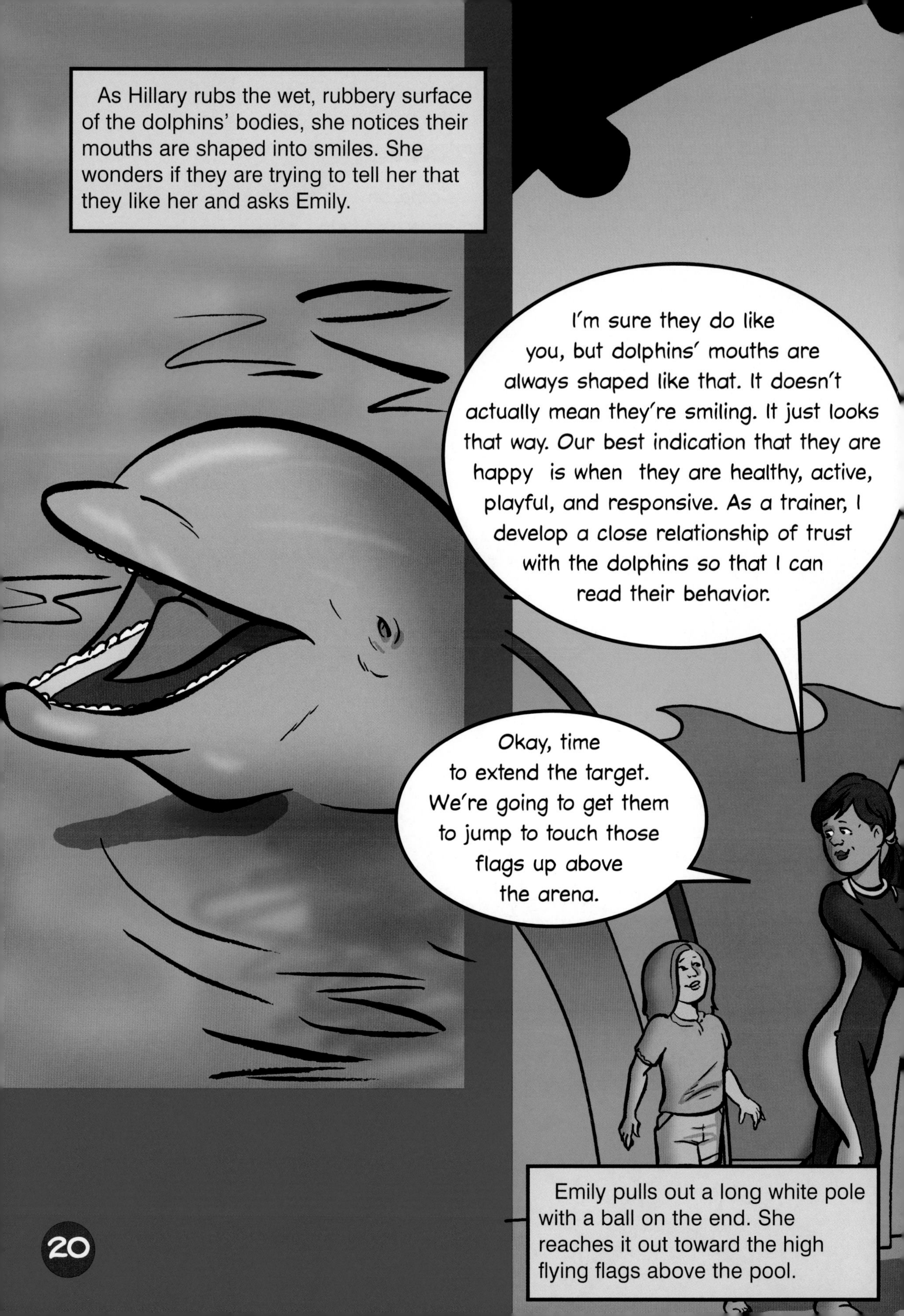

As Hillary rubs the wet, rubbery surface of the dolphins' bodies, she notices their mouths are shaped into smiles. She wonders if they are trying to tell her that they like her and asks Emily.

I'm sure they do like you, but dolphins' mouths are always shaped like that. It doesn't actually mean they're smiling. It just looks that way. Our best indication that they are happy is when they are healthy, active, playful, and responsive. As a trainer, I develop a close relationship of trust with the dolphins so that I can read their behavior.

Okay, time to extend the target. We're going to get them to jump to touch those flags up above the arena.

Emily pulls out a long white pole with a ball on the end. She reaches it out toward the high flying flags above the pool.

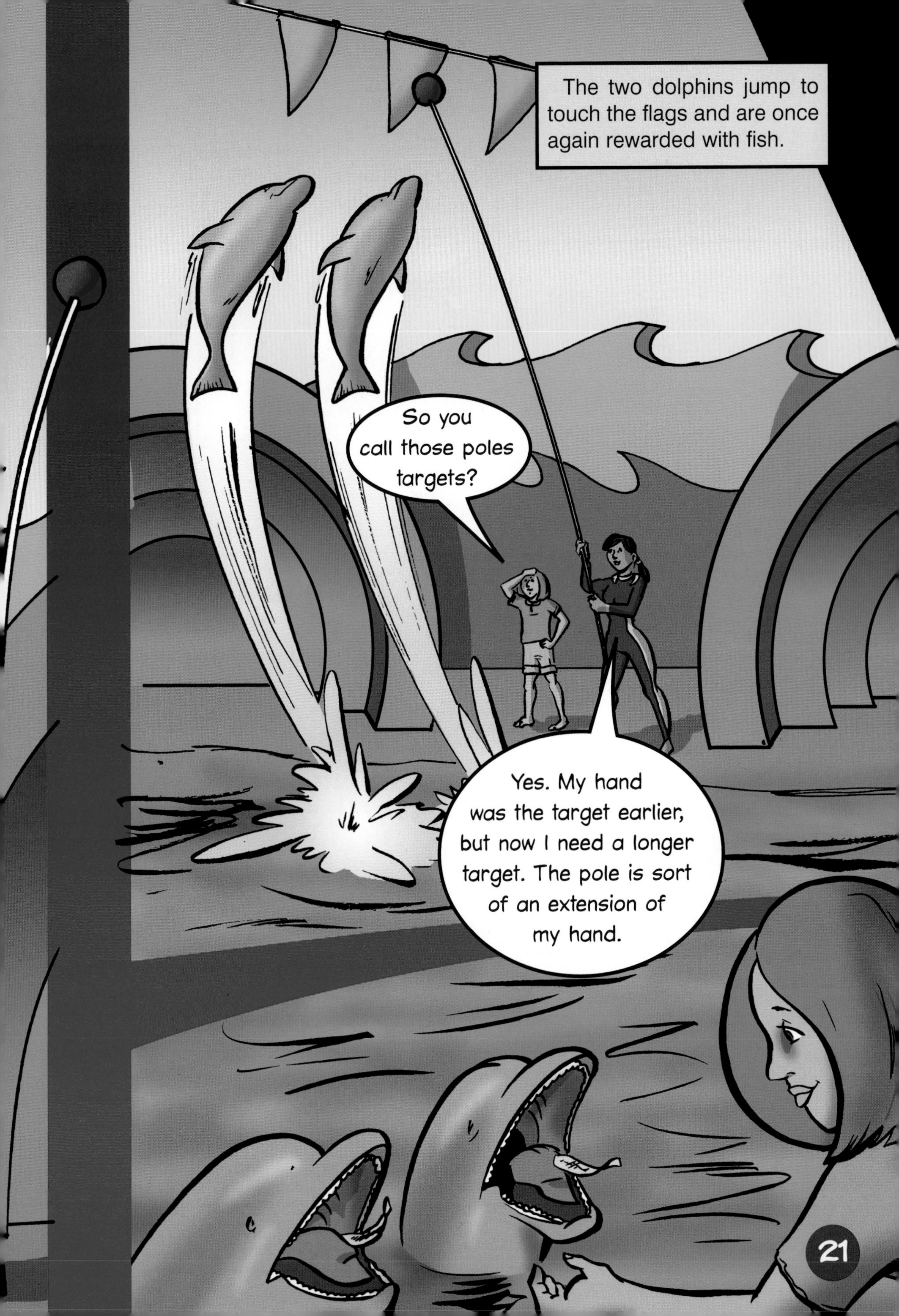

The two dolphins jump to touch the flags and are once again rewarded with fish.
So you call those poles targets?
Yes. My hand was the target earlier, but now I need a longer target. The pole is sort of an extension of my hand.

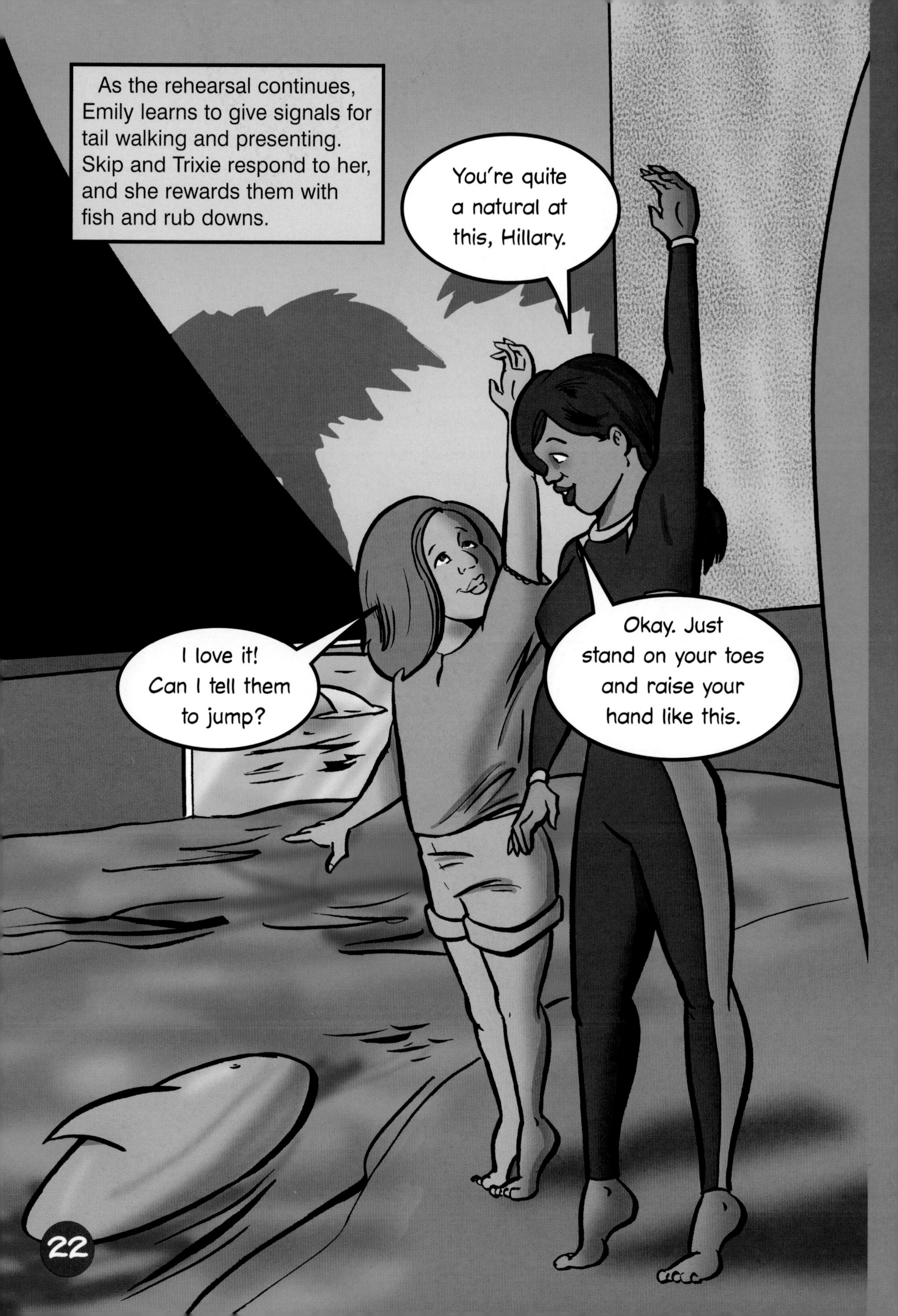
As the rehearsal continues, Emily learns to give signals for tail walking and presenting. Skip and Trixie respond to her, and she rewards them with fish and rub downs.
You're quite a natural at this, Hillary.
I love it! Can I tell them to jump?
Okay. Just stand on your toes and raise your hand like this.

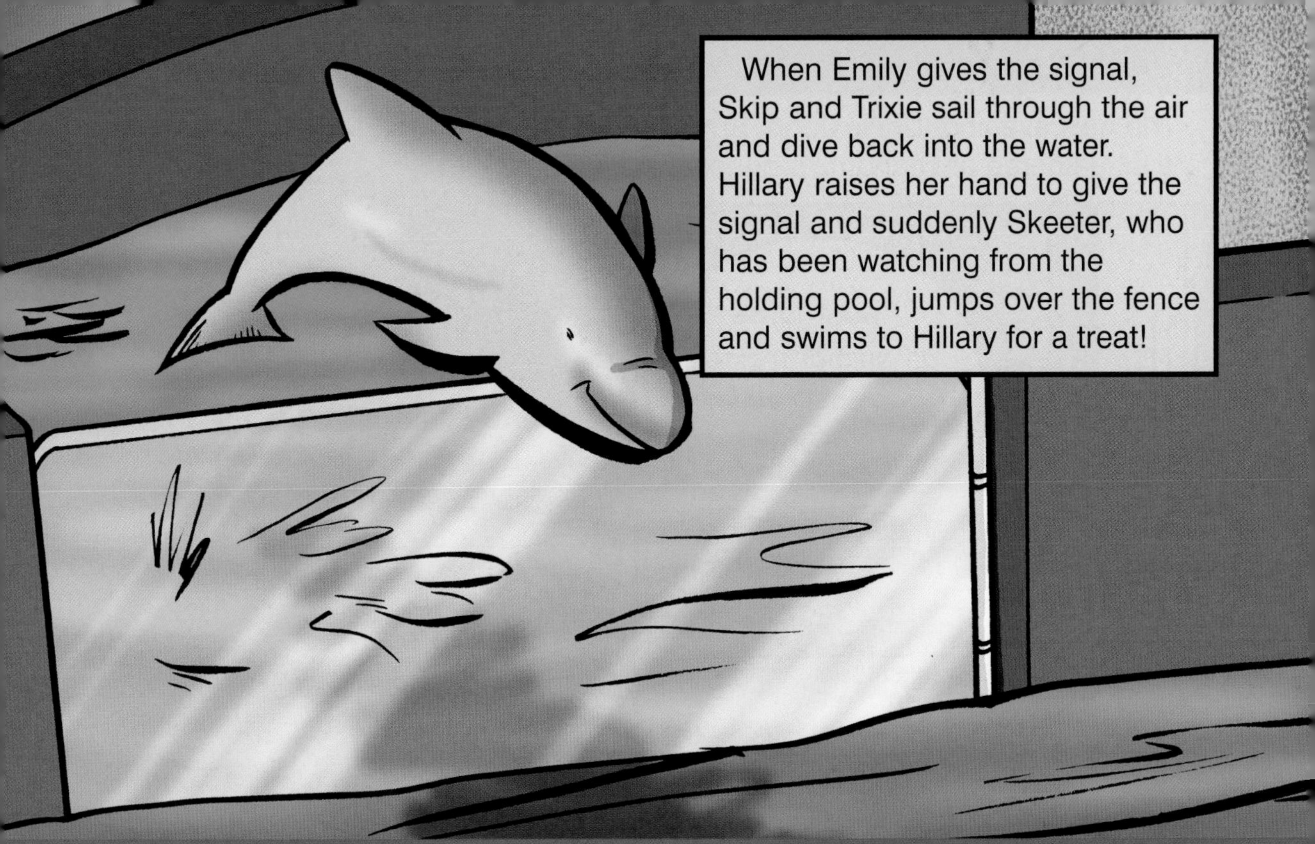
When Emily gives the signal, Skip and Trixie sail through the air and dive back into the water. Hillary raises her hand to give the signal and suddenly Skeeter, who has been watching from the holding pool, jumps over the fence and swims to Hillary for a treat!

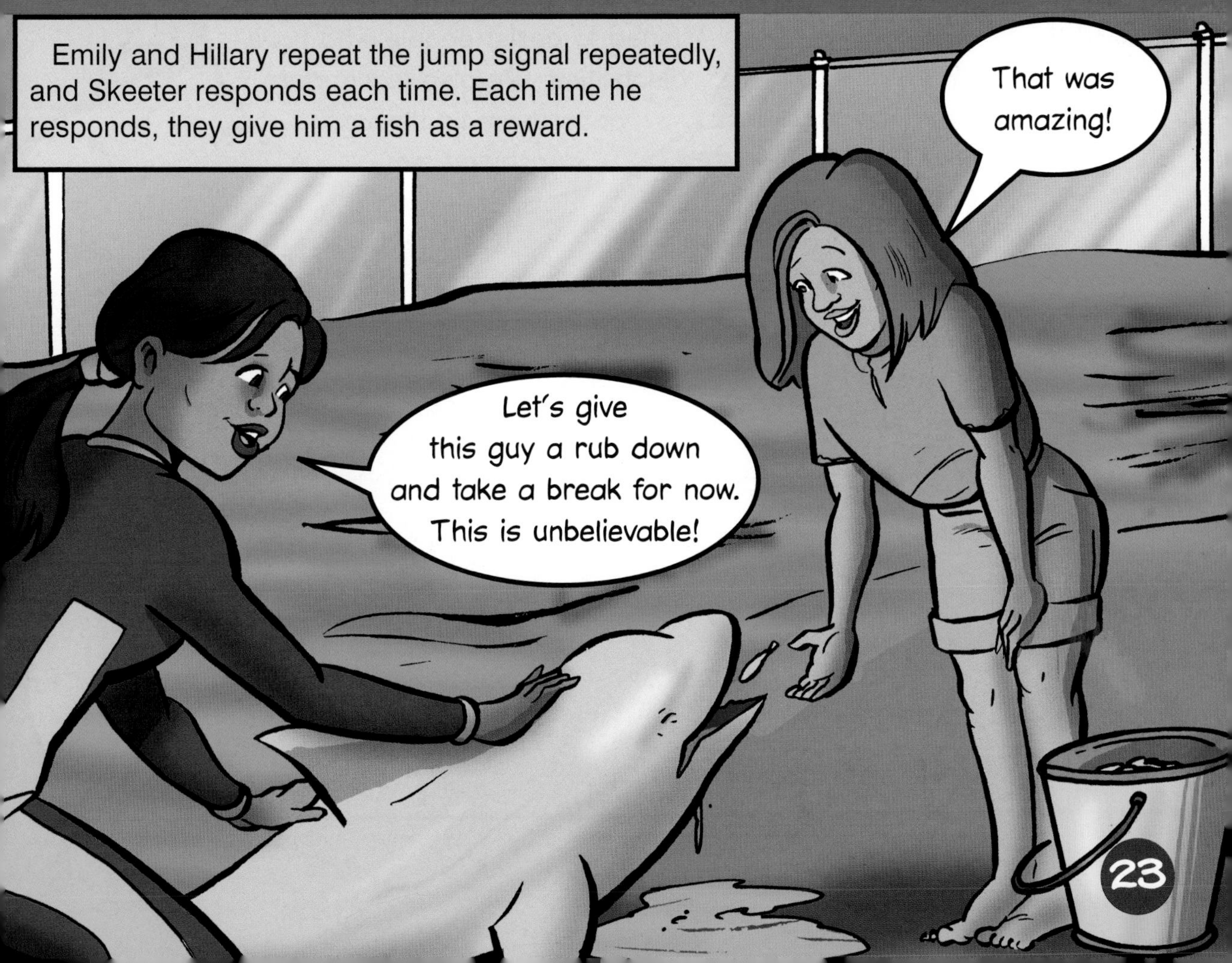
Emily and Hillary repeat the jump signal repeatedly, and Skeeter responds each time. Each time he responds, they give him a fish as a reward.
That was amazing!
Let's give this guy a rub down and take a break for now. This is unbelievable!

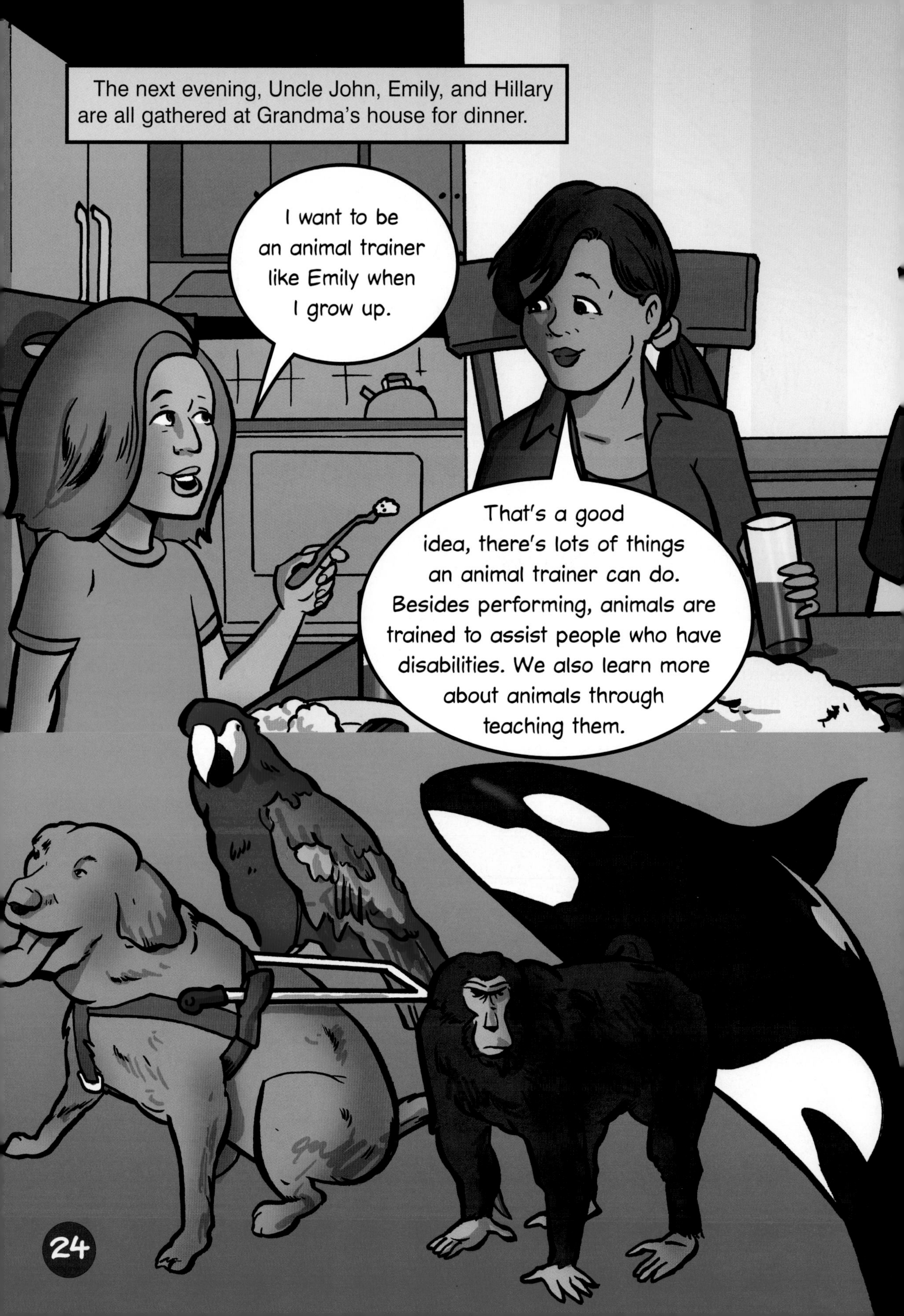

The next evening, Uncle John, Emily, and Hillary are all gathered at Grandma's house for dinner.
I want to be an animal trainer like Emily when I grow up.
That's a good idea, there's lots of things an animal trainer can do. Besides performing, animals are trained to assist people who have disabilities. We also learn more about animals through teaching them.

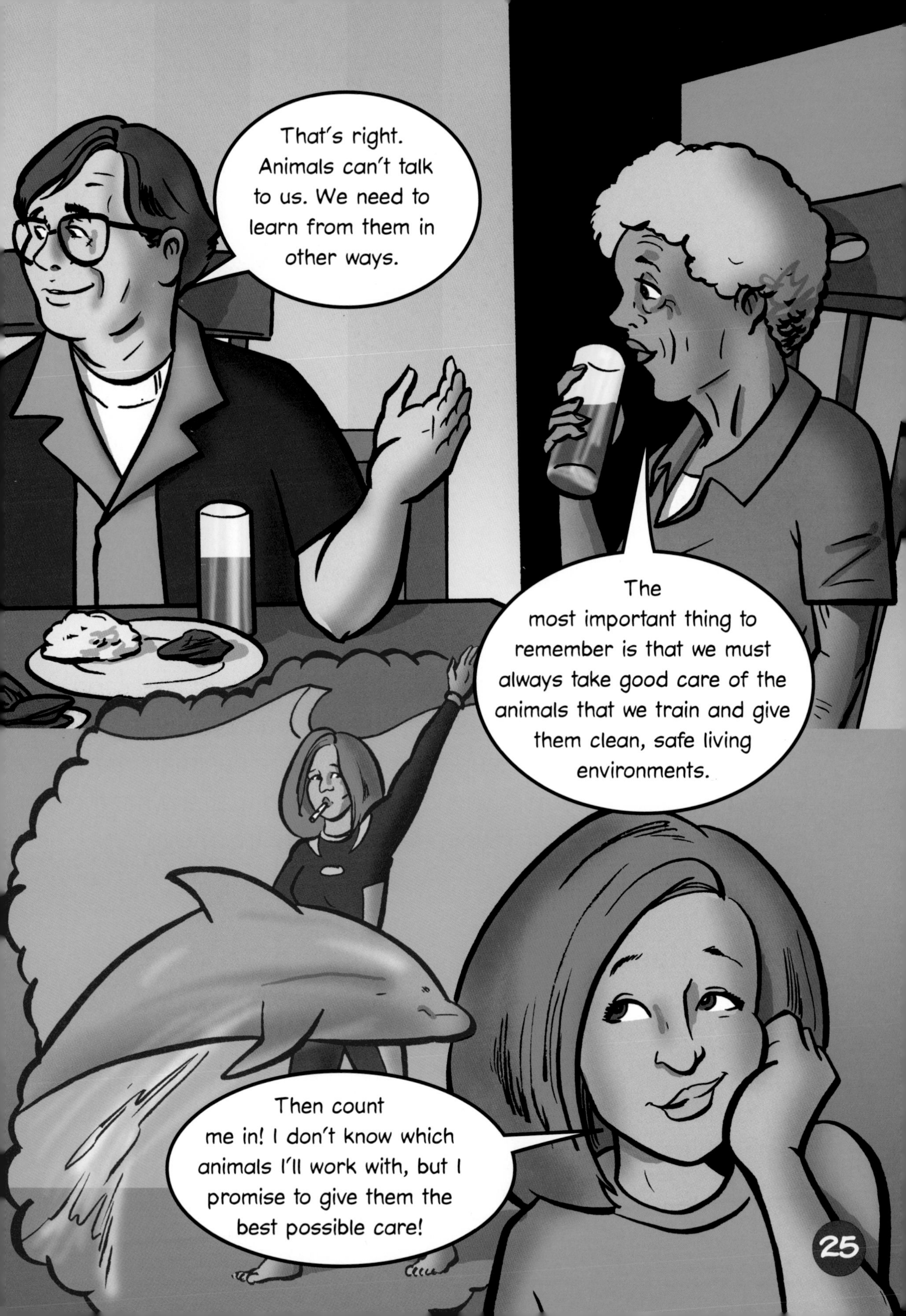
That's right. Animals can't talk to us. We need to learn from them in other ways.
The most important thing to remember is that we must always take good care of the animals that we train and give them clean, safe living environments.
Then count me in! I don't know which animals I'll work with, but I promise to give them the best possible care!

Animal Training

Animal training involves teaching animals to respond in a desired way when a command is given. Trainers use a system of

rewards and punishments to shape animals' responses. Animal trainers must have a strong understanding of animal behavior and good communication skills. Usually, animal trainers work with animals and people.

The most commonly trained animals are dogs, horses, and marine mammals. Sometimes they are trained to perform tricks on film or in front of a live audience. Sometimes animals are trained to assist a person who is disabled. No matter what the purpose, people who train animals must treat them with patience and respect.

Marine Mammals

Many marine mammals, like bottlenose dolphins, killer whales, and sea lions, are trained to entertain audiences. Trainers want the audience to focus on the animal. Therefore, they usually use hand signs instead of voice commands. When marine mammals perform, they are rewarded with positive praise, food, or a rub-down.

Working Animals

Animals are trained to work for police and fire departments, airport security, and ski resorts. One of the most important tasks a dog does for the police is to sniff out illegal drugs. They are trained to alert their handlers when they smell drugs by pawing at the ground or barking. Fire departments and ski resorts use dogs that are trained to find people who need rescuing. Airport security uses dogs to sniff out drugs and bombs. Instead of pawing at the ground, they are trained to sit next to the area where they smell the bomb. They are also trained to identify vegetables and fruit that are being smuggled into the country. When working dogs are successful in their jobs, they learn that they will be rewarded with treats and playtime.

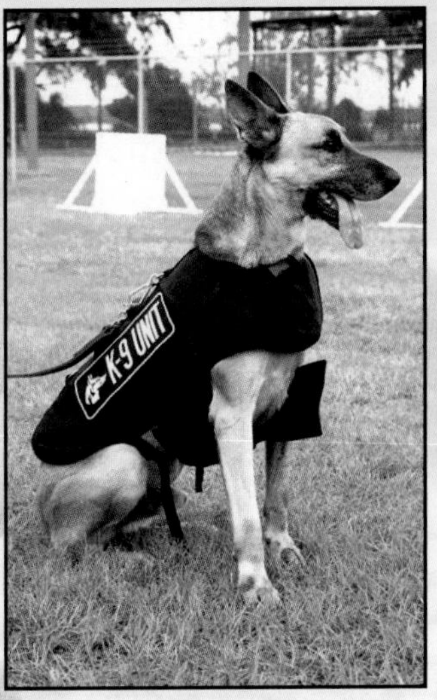
K-9 UNIT
Police K-9 Dog.

Therapy Animals

Many animals, especially dogs, are trained to be therapy animals. Therapy animals, such as dogs, cats, and rabbits, are often regular visitors to hospitals and nursing homes. Usually these animal volunteers are a family pet whose owner has taken a pet-therapy training course and takes their pet to different places.

Children with autism or other disorders that make communication difficult may work with a therapy dog or other animal to help them build communication skills. Sometimes these therapy animals live and work with one companion, while other therapy animals may work with many different children that come to a center for therapy once or twice a week.

It's important to remember that not all animals have the personality to be a therapy animal. Therapy animals need to be calm animals that like being around lots of people.

Service Animals

Animals are often trained to help people with **disabilities**. When we think of service animals, we usually think of guide dogs that assist people who are visually impaired or blind. It might surprise you to find out that many different types of animals, such as miniature horses, monkeys, parrots, dogs, cats, and goats, are also trained to be service animals and they aren't just trained as guide animals. Service animals can be trained to do everything from alerting a person before they have a seizure to picking up things for someone who has limited **mobility**.

People who are visually impaired often have a guide dog to help them avoid objects and assist them in crossing streets safely.

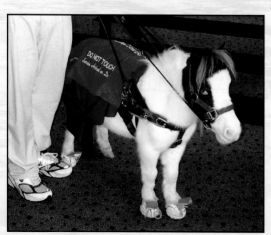

Miniature horses are becoming a popular alternative to guide dogs. One of the many benefits of having a guide horse is its lifespan. Miniature horses can live over 50 years and are good companions for 30 to 40 years. Since dogs have a shorter lifespan, they usually retire after 8 to 12 years of service. And yes, guide horses are housebroken too!

Learning to be an Animal Trainer

Most animal training jobs require some kind of education and certification. Many people attend community colleges and vocational schools to learn the skills needed for training animals. Some animal training jobs, like working with marine mammals, require college degrees.

Many organizations offer workshops to help people learn to work with their own pets or with animals in their community. The Humane Society of the United States, the American Humane Association, and the National Animal Control Association are three organizations that help people learn to work with animals in a positive way.

Glossary

arena (uh-REE-nuh): An area where animals perform.

assistance (uh-SIS-tuhnss): The help that is supplied.

disabilities (DIS-uh-bil-uh-teez): Physical problems, such as blindness or an inability to hear.

husbandry (HUHZ-buhnd-ree): The production and care of domestic animals.

mobility (MOH-bil-i-tee): The ability to move or be moved. When a person has limited mobility, he is not able to move his arms or legs completely.

operant conditioning (OP-er-ant kuhn-DISH-uhn-ing): Training a person or an animal to repeat a desired behavior by rewarding the subject with a reward or a treat when the behavior occurs. This reinforces the behavior and makes it occur again.

reinforcement (ree-in-FORSS-muhnt): Something that strengthens something else by using additional assistance, material, or support.

veterinarian (vet-ur-uh-NER-ee-uhn): A doctor who treats sick or injured animals.

Index

Websites

www.animaltraining.org

www.seaworld.org/animal-info/infobooks/training/index.htm

www.humanesocietyyouth.org

www.guidehorse.org

www.deltasociety.org

About the Author

Susan Koehler is a teacher and a writer who lives in Tallahassee, Florida. As a child, she loved reading mysteries. She liked books so much that she gave up her recess time in elementary school to work in the school library. Beyond the pages of books, she enjoyed listening to stories about the colorful, real-life experiences of her parents and older siblings. Now she lives in a busy house filled with books, animals, and very funny children.

About the Artist

After graduating from the Joe Kubert School of Cartoon and Graphic Art, Thom Zahler began his ten-year career as a caricaturist at an amusement park. Later, Zahler began drawing cartoons and other silly pictures for clients such as the Cleveland Indians, the Colorado Rockies, and the Rock and Roll Hall of Fame. He has also worked for Marvel Comics, DC Comics, and Warner Brothers International. Zahler currently writes and draws Love and Capes, a romantic comedy comic book. Zahler lives in Timberlake, Ohio. He works from his house, frequently in his pajamas, and always with a cup of coffee.